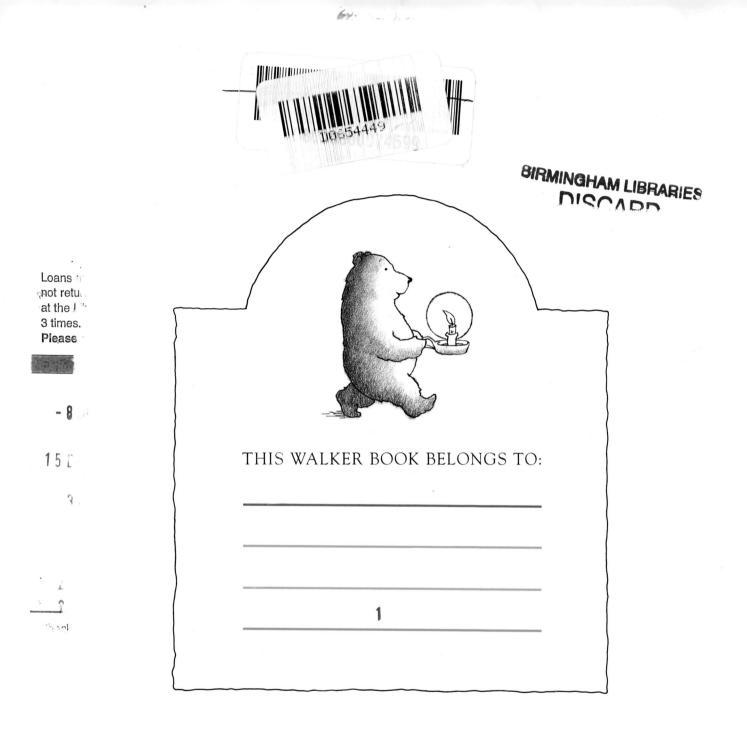

THIS WALKER BOOK BELONGS TO:

_____

_____

1

_____

Squeak's
Good Idea

For Tom and Danny
∽ M.E.

For Alexander Agnew
P.B. ∽

First published 2001 by Walker Books Ltd
87 Vauxhall Walk, London SE11 5HJ

This edition published 2002

10 9 8 7 6 5 4 3 2 1

Text © 2001 Max Eilenberg
Illustrations © 2001 Patrick Benson

The right of Max Eilenberg to be identified as author of this work
has been asserted by him in accordance with the Copyright, Designs and Patents Act 1988

This book has been typeset in Minion Condensed

Printed in Hong Kong

British Library Cataloguing in Publication Data:
a catalogue record for this book is available from the British Library

ISBN 0-7445-8936-3

Squeak's
Good Idea

Words by **Max Eilenberg**

Pictures by **Patrick Benson**

WALKER BOOKS
AND SUBSIDIARIES
LONDON • BOSTON • SYDNEY

"I've got a good idea," said Squeak.

"Let's all go out. Who wants to come?"

"I'm a bit busy," said Poppa.

Momma and Tumble were busy too.

"Oh," said Squeak.
"Then I'll have
to go on my own."

He opened the door
and looked out.
"Hmm," he said.
"It might be cold."

So he went to the cupboard
and fetched his coat.

And then, just to be on the safe
side, he got his mittens, his hat
and his warmest trousers as well.

"Momma," he called.

"Can I borrow your scarf?"

"Of course you can,"
said Momma.

Squeak went back to the door.

He looked out.

"Hmm," he said.

"It might rain."

So he went to the hall and fetched
his mac. And then, just to be
on the safe side, he got his
wellington boots and some
extra socks as well.

"Poppa," he called.

"Can I borrow
your umbrella?"

"Of course you can,"
said Poppa.

Squeak went back to the door.

He looked out.

"Hmm," he said.

"I might get hungry."

So he went to the kitchen
and fetched some biscuits.
And then, just to be on the safe side,
he got some bread and some apples
and a basket to carry them in.
"What are you doing?" asked Tumble.

"I thought," said Squeak,
"I might have a picnic."

Squeak went back to the door.

He looked out.

"Hmm," he said.

"I'm ready."

Squeak stepped outside.

"That's a pretty flower," he said.

"What a noisy bee."

Squeak walked, one step at a time,

to the tree at the end of the garden.

"Hmm," said Squeak.
  He put down his basket.
"It's not at all cold – and
  it's certainly not rainy."

So he pulled off his
wellington boots,
and his extra socks,
and his mac and his coat,
and his warmest trousers,
and his mittens and his hat,
and he tied Momma's scarf
to Poppa's umbrella
and he hung them
from the tree.

"Good," said Squeak.

He looked at his basket.

"Now it's time for my…"

"**P I C N I C !**" yelled Tumble.

"I'm glad you've come," said Squeak.

"This was a good idea," said Momma.

"I love picnics!" said Tumble.

"Lucky you brought so many things,"
   said Poppa.

"Hmm," said Squeak. "It's best
   to be on the safe side."

And everyone agreed
that it was.

Max Eilenberg says of *Squeak's Good Idea*, "When you're little –
or even big – doing something on your own is exciting but also scary.
You think of every reason you can for dawdling."

Max is also the author of *Cowboy Kid*, illustrated by Sue Heap. He enjoys
playing music and football with his two sons, and lives in London with his family.

Patrick Benson says of *Squeak's Good Idea*, "Squeak reminds me of
myself when I set off fishing! I go from cupboard to cupboard collecting
things 'just in case'. I end up completely laden down and certain
that I've forgotten the most important thing!"

Patrick has illustrated many well-loved picture books, including
Owl Babies by Martin Waddell; Russell Hoban's *The Sea-thing Child*,
which won the National Art Library Illustration Award; and *The Little Boat* by
Kathy Henderson, which was Highly Commended for the Kate Greenaway Medal,
shortlisted for the Smarties Book Prize and Winner of the Kurt Maschler Award.
He lives in Roxburghshire, Scotland, with his family.

ISBN 0-7445-8200-8 (pb)

ISBN 0-7445-3167-5 (pb)

ISBN 0-7445-7826-4 (pb)